For Douglas

Copyright © 2020 by Holly Hobbie

All rights reserved. Published in the United States by Random House Children's Books,
a division of Penguin Random House LLC, New York.

Random House and the colophon are registered trademarks
of Penguin Random House LLC.

Visit us on the Web! rhcbooks.com

Educators and librarians, for a variety of teaching tools,
visit us at RHTeachersLibrarians.com

Library of Congress Cataloging-in-Publication Data is available upon request.
ISBN 978-1-5247-7081-5 (trade) — ISBN 978-1-5247-7082-2 (lib. bdg.) — ISBN 978-1-5247-7083-9 (ebook)

MANUFACTURED IN CHINA
10 9 8 7 6 5 4 3 2 1
First Edition

Holly Hobbie

ELMORE
and
Pinky

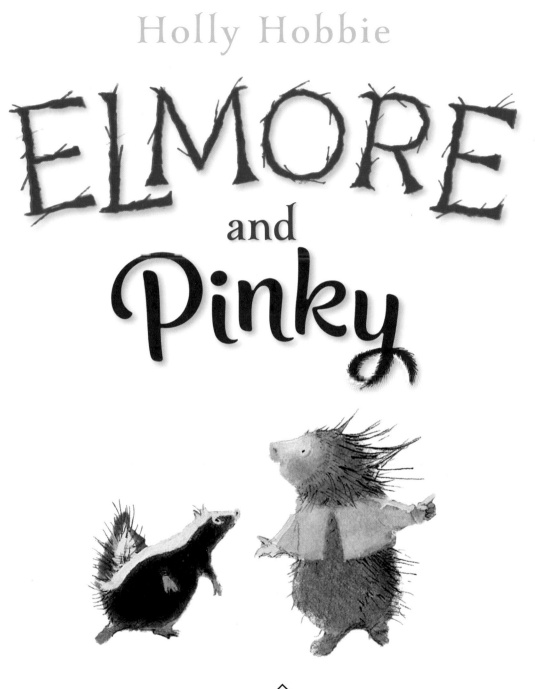

Random House New York

Elmore had plenty of friends. He lived alone, but he wasn't lonely. He seldom left his dwelling without being greeted by a pleasant neighbor. It gave him a warm feeling. Still, he felt something was missing–a best friend, he thought.

"A companion," his uncle suggested, helping Elmore over a big word.

"Yes, a companion," Elmore repeated. "That's exactly what I mean. Having a bunch of friendly neighbors is not the same as having a best friend."

Elmore thought this over, then asked, "How do you get one?"

"It just happens," his uncle told him. "You'll know."

One afternoon while Elmore was enjoying a sunny moment, Pinky the skunk came waddling along.

"What a beautiful day, Elmore. Can I join you?" asked Pinky.

"Please do," said Elmore.

"I hear you are looking for a best friend. How will you find one?" Pinky asked.

"According to my uncle, it just happens."

"Well, if you're nocturnal, your best friend would have to stay up all night, too," whispered Pinky.

"Definitely," Elmore agreed. "He might be out in the woods right now."

"It's not happening," Elmore admitted to his uncle. "There don't seem to be any spare best friends around."

"Maybe you're looking too hard," his uncle suggested. "Be patient. There is a best friend for everyone."

The next day, while Elmore was contentedly picking blueberries, a bear cub came tumbling toward him, eager to play.

"Stay back!" Elmore cried. "You'll get stuck with my quills. Stay back!"

But the cub kept coming, running circles around Elmore.

"Help!" Elmore shouted.

With a sudden great commotion, the mother bear burst through some branches. Nothing was more fierce, Elmore knew, than a mother bear protecting her cub.

"Help!" he shouted louder than before. Responding to danger, his body arched into a prickly ball. "Help!"

Then he saw Pinky enter the fray, and
an unmistakable scent filled the air.

"Pinky," cried Elmore, "is that you?"
Snatching up her cub, the mother
bear vanished into the woods.

"You were so brave," Elmore said. "You saved me."

"Bears can't stand the smell of skunk," Pinky said. "It makes them faint."

"I like it," Elmore told him. "It's so you."

Elmore's blueberry pie came out beautifully, but this was where the best friend came in. More than half the pleasure of a blueberry pie was sharing it. He couldn't wait for Pinky to taste it.

Elmore suddenly paused. Yes, he definitely wanted Pinky to be the first to taste it. What did that mean? he asked himself.

Pinky was grooming himself near the old fallen birch tree he lived in.

"You're so clever and kind," Elmore told him. "Why don't you have a special friend?"

"No one wants to be best friends with a skunk," Pinky said. "I stink."

"Only in emergencies," Elmore said. "But guess what—I've found my best friend! He was right under my nose all along."

"I can't wait to meet him," said Pinky.

"It's you!" Elmore exclaimed. "That is, if you'd like me to be your best friend, too."

"It just happened—like you said it would,"
Elmore told his uncle.

"You make a pair," the uncle told them.

"I love being nocturnal," Elmore said.
Pinky agreed.